CASE OF THE
MISSING CAKE

By Daniel Mauleón

SCHOLASTIC INC.

CASE OF THE
MISSING CAKE

©2022 Viacom International Inc. All Rights Reserved. Nickelodeon, The Casagrandes and all related titles, logos, and characters are trademarks of Viacom International Inc.

All rights reserved. Published by Scholastic Inc., *Publishers since 1920.* SCHOLASTIC and associated logos are trademarks and/or registered trademarks of Scholastic Inc.

ISBN 978-1-338-77554-9

10 9 8 7 6 5 4 3 2 1   22 23 24 25 26
Printed in the U.S.A.   40
First printing 2022

1

EL GALLO ROJO PUFFS UP his chest and crows. The luchador, dressed like a rooster, leaps onto the ropes of the ring. He springs off and into the air, flying at—

"Bobby!" I shout at my older brother as he blocks my view of the TV. It's bad enough that I have to watch from the kitchen.

"Oh, sorry, Ronnie Anne," he says, grabbing one of Abuela's flautas. "I needed

a restock." He shoves it into his mouth and steps away. Finally, I can see the TV again.

"Ah man! I missed his signature move!"

"Mija—are you helping, or are you watching?" my abuela replies.

"Oh. Sorry, Abuela." I turn away from the TV and back to the task at hand. My abuela, my mom's mother, has a mixing bowl tucked in her left arm and an old recipe card in her left hand. She reads from the card to me while she stirs the contents of the bowl with her right hand. It's no wrestling move, but it is a pretty impressive maneuver.

"While I'm mixing the wet ingredients, I need you to sift the flour, cocoa, baking soda, baking powder, and salt!"

I pour the ingredients one by one into a sifter, holding it carefully above a mixing bowl. Then I get to sifting, shaking the different parts together. They settle in the bowl below.

I live with my mom, brother, and grand-parents in an apartment building, and my aunt, uncle, and cousins live there, too. (So does my best friend!) It can get wild, but it's fun—life here is never dull, that's for sure!

Anyway, tomorrow night is our build-ing's annual summer party. Each tenant is supposed to bring something special to share. I kept joking that I would bring myself, but no one found that as funny as I did. That's when Abuela asked if I wanted to help her make her famous tres leches cake, saying that we could bring it together. I agreed right away—Abuela is a fantastic cook, and her tres leches is delicious, so I knew that meant I'd be bringing one of the best things to the party! As long as I didn't mess it up.

Of course, when I agreed, I thought we would be making the cake the day of the party, but Abuela insisted it must be made the night before. So now I'm stuck in the kitchen helping her bake instead of watching all the Lucha Libre action in the living room with the rest of my family. And to make things even worse, my favorite luchadora, La Tormenta, is scheduled to fight tonight!

I start sifting faster, but that just makes a cloud of flour puff into my face.

"Mamá," says my tío Carlos—my mom's brother—with a groan. He pokes his head sideways past the kitchen door, grimacing in pain.

"What's the matter, mijo?" Abuela asks. "Why are you all sideways? Stand up straight."

"About that . . ." Carlos says as he walks completely through the doorway. His back is bent backward at about a ninety-degree angle.

"Whoa!" Abuela and I shout in unison.

Two of my cousins, Carl and CJ, walk into the kitchen behind Carlos. They're both wearing Lucha masks. I have a suspicion about what just happened.

"We were practicing some new moves," Carl says casually.

"We got a *little* carried away," CJ explains, with much more concern than his brother.

"No worries, Carlos," Abuela says, placing her mixing bowl on the counter and walking to the bathroom. Within seconds she's back with a small blue tub of vapor rub.

Abuela grabs a handful of the blue, jelly-like rub and flings it down the back of Tío Carlos's collar. It smells like mouthwash, and I have no clue how it works, but of all of Abuela's special remedies, vapor rub is the one I trust most.

Carlos shakes for a second. "That kind

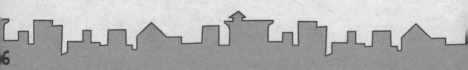

of tickles!" he says. Then he breathes a sigh as the vapor rub works its magic.

"Now, let's set you right!" Abuela says, lifting Tío Carlos from the ground and straightening him up again with a *CRACK!*

"Thanks, Mamá," Carlos says, and he, Carl, and CJ head back into the living room. As soon as they're out of sight, Carl gives a battle cry, and I hear Carlos yell, "*Yeowch!*" I just shake my head.

"How's the sifting, Ronnie Anne?" Abuela asks. I look down at the pile of dry ingredients, which doesn't look too different than when I began.

"Uh, good, I think?"

"Perfecto! Now we'll add the secret

ingredient." Just as Abuela reaches into the cabinet, there's a loud cheer from the living room. I whip my head back toward the TV. What did I miss?!

"Yeah, you show them who's the boss!" my abuelo—my grandfather—calls from the couch. I try to see the TV to find out who "the boss" is, but Bobby is blocking my view.

While I try to find the right angle, I can hear Abuela moving around me in the kitchen. "This recipe has a long history in this family, Ronnie Anne. My mother, Mamá Lupe, made this cake many, many times. For birthdays and quinces, and sometimes just because."

"Uh-huh," I say, nodding. I'm listening,

even if I'm not paying *full* attention.

"But this special ingredient was a mistake," Abuela continues. "When Mamá Lupe made this to celebrate my twelfth birthday, her parrot, Paco, got a taste of the batter. He zipped around the kitchen in excitement, knocking in just a little bit of this."

"WOW!" I shout as I catch a glimpse of El Gallo Rojo getting tossed out of the ring. Thankfully, Abuela thinks I'm commenting on her story.

"WOW, indeed!" she continues. "We all thought the flavor would ruin the cake, but Mamá went ahead and baked it, and to our surprise, the amazing recipe got even better!" After a pause, she adds, "And then we all sprouted wings and flew around the house."

"Sounds cool, Abuela."

"Ronnie Anne . . ." Abuela says, her tone carrying her judgment.

Busted. It's true that I wasn't *quite* paying attention to her. "Sorry, Abuela," I say, and reluctantly turn back to her and the cake. "What's next?"

"Mix the wet and dry ingredients—"

"Can do!"

"And keep your eye on the bowl, not the TV."

"Yes, Abuela."

While I stir, Abuela greases a metal cake pan, and we are interrupted by my prima Carlota—my cousin. She's CJ and Carl's older sister, and is way cool.

"Thanks again for letting me borrow your earrings, Abuela! Retro is really in right now," Carlota says, showing off some pearl earrings.

"Of course, dear," Abuela says warmly, admiring Carlota. "My fashion is timeless. If you're lucky, those earrings will even help win you a cute admirer."

Yuck, I think. Though I'm not sure Carlota agrees with me.

"Abuela!" she says. "I'm just hanging out with my friends."

"You never know," Abuela says slyly as she hugs Carlota goodbye.

Next, Abuela guides me as I pour the mixed batter into the pan. She shakes the pan to settle the batter and tosses it into the oven to bake. Meanwhile, I dip my finger into the batter left in the bowl and have a taste. BAM! It's spicy! Delicious, but definitely surprising. Just what *is* that special ingredient?

"Oooh, tres leches batter!" says Sergio, Abuela's parrot, as he perches on the pass-through ledge. A moment later, Lalo, our really big dog, pops his head up, too, his tongue dripping drool. Finally, Carlitos, my baby primo—the littlest cousin—climbs up Lalo and onto the counter.

"Uh-uh, none for you," Abuela says sternly. Carlitos, Sergio, and Lalo all give her hungry puppy eyes (which is especially easy for Lalo, since he's a dog).

Abuela lets out a sigh. "No batter, but I'll fix you up a snack." She opens the fridge and starts digging around for a meal fit for the odd trio.

I look into the oven as the cake begins to bake. "You know, Abuela, it's a good thing I'm helping you out. With everyone coming in and needing your assistance, it would have taken you a long time to make this. You really hold this family together."

Abuela's head is still in the fridge, but she can see right through me. "Yes, Ronnie Anne," she says, "you can go watch the show."

I manage a quick "Thanks, Abuela!" then dash into the living room to catch the next match.

2

TO MY GREAT DISAPPOINTMENT, La Tormenta won't be fighting until the final match. But any Lucha is better than no Lucha. So I cheer along during the fight. However, before they announce a winner, Abuela calls me back into the kitchen.

Abuela doesn't see me roll my eyes, but my mom does. She's dressed in her scrubs, ready to go to work at the hospital—but it seems she has just enough time for a lecture before she leaves. "Ronnie Anne, remember you're lucky your abuela is letting you help out. You don't want to be empty-handed at the party tomorrow."

"And what are you bringing?" I ask.

"I'm bringing myself!" She laughs. My jaw drops to the floor. That was *my* idea!

My mom continues, "I'll be lucky if I can even catch some sleep between this shift and the party. Ronnie Anne, this is a great time for you to pick up some of Abuela's cooking skills and spend some quality time with her."

That's the end of it. Mom gets up and

walks me to the kitchen before kissing me goodbye on the forehead.

In the kitchen, Abuela hands me a mixing bowl and spatula.

"Wait. Why are we still mixing? Are we making frosting?" I ask.

"You are mixing the tres leches," Abuela says. She gestures to the counter, where there are two cans and a carton of heavy cream. "Open up those cans of milk and mix them with the cream."

"*Canned* milk?" I didn't even know that was a thing.

"Yes, mija. Now get to it! The cake is almost ready."

I open the cans. One is labeled EVAPORATED MILK, and I almost expect the can to be empty. The other is condensed milk, a name that sounds like it should be some sort of yogurt. But when I pour them both into the bowl, they simply look like . . . milk? I add a cup of heavy cream and stir them together. Three milks. Tres leches. *Ohhhh*, now I get it.

Abuela opens the oven and brings out the cake, setting it on the counter next to me.

"Here you go, mija," she says, handing me a toothpick. "We need to poke some holes in the top for the tres leches."

I follow her lead and start poking the cake. It's *very* relaxing, and my mind starts to drift back to Lucha. Maybe if I work fast enough, I can catch the finale.

"Uh, mija," Abuela says, looking at the cake, "something on your mind?" I look down and see I've poked holes in the shape of La Tormenta's face. Oops!

Abuela passes me the bowl of tres leches.

"Okay, now pour it on the cake."

"What?!" Is this really how tres leches is made?!

"Trust me, Ronnie Anne, this is where the recipe comes together and makes the cake special."

I grab the bowl and carefully pour it over the cake, and the tres leches pools on top of the pan. Honestly, it looks like cake soup.

"Now watch," Abuela says. It takes a moment, but the tres leches mixture starts to soak into the cake through the tiny holes and around the edges. The cake almost seems to shine. There is still a bit pooled around the edges of the pan, but the cake has soaked up most of it. Abuela was right; this is magic.

Abuela takes out some plastic wrap and covers up the pan and cake in a tight seal. "We will let it sit overnight in the fridge and give the cake time to absorb all the sweetness from the tres leches. Then tomorrow, I'll top it with some whipped cream, and it will be ready for the party."

Abuela tucks the cake in the fridge, and I realize we're all done.

Then I realize I had entirely forgotten about Lucha! At least for a moment.

"Can I watch the rest of the show now?" I ask.

"I still need you for one more very important task," Abuela says, and I let out a sigh. "Your tía Frida needs me as a model for a new series of portraits, so I'm heading next door. I need you to watch the cake and make sure no one tries to eat it. Especially not Sergio. Not after *the incident* . . . But that's a story for another evening. I'm off!"

"Okay, Abuela, I'll watch," I say, resigned. I'll at least have a view of the show from here, even if it's partially blocked by Bobby.

Abuela waves goodbye and heads across the hall to my tía Frida and tío Carlos's apartment. I grab the broom and prop myself up on a pasta strainer on a chair in the kitchen. That makes me look more official in my role as tres leches guard, and gives me some added height to watch the show.

Soon, Abuelo steps into the kitchen. When he makes a move for the fridge, I point the broom at him. "I'm watching you, Abuelo," I warn him. He opens the refrigerator slowly and, without breaking eye contact with me, grabs some leftover tamales. Then he hurries out of the kitchen. And after that, my watch goes quiet.

I look out into the living room, where my family is still watching the show. Then I see her. La Tormenta takes the ring, in all her thundering glory! And then Bobby's big head blocks my view again.

I look at the fridge and the empty kitchen. Then I look at my family around the TV. I figure I don't need to watch the cake if I can watch them. So I set down my broom and lean in to catch the final Lucha Libre match.

★ ★ ★

I wake up the next morning exhausted. During La Tormenta's match, I cheered so loud that my throat is now sore. I drag myself out of bed and to the kitchen. Hopefully, some orange juice will help.

But when I open the fridge, the rest of the night comes crashing back. Oh no.

After Lucha, I went straight to my room to practice some moves on my pillows, and forgot entirely about my guard duty. And now the tres leches cake is . . . MISSING.

3

I OPEN THE FRIDGE. Then close it. Then open it again. I'm practically willing the universe to make the cake reappear. But it's gone. Vanished. Nonexistent. I consider lighting one of Abuela's candles and praying to whichever saint is in charge of cakes to return it to me. But I'm not sure if there is even a saint for that—and anyway, I'm not allowed to use matches.

Instead, I sneak back to my room and plant my face into my pillow. I want to scream, but even with a pillow muffling the sound, I don't want to alert Abuela.

Bzzzt! My phone rings on my bedside table, and I roll my head over to check the screen. It's a new text from Dad. I flop my arm onto the phone to open the text.

Hey, Ranita, it begins. That's his nickname for me. It means "little frog." My mind wanders. How freeing it would be to be a little frog right now . . . Little frogs don't have cake-watching responsibilities. They just need to hop around. Well, hop around and not get eaten by birds. I wonder what would be worse,

25

being eaten by a bird or being chewed out by Abuela. I'd prefer the bird.

I read my dad's full text.

Hey, Ranita, your mom invited me to the party tonight. Not sure what to bring. Got an idea?

Any other day, I would be happy about a wake-up text from my dad. But there's no way I can be responsible for what he's bringing to the party—I'm too stressed about what I'm bringing already! Once I handle the tres leches, then I can lend him a hand. Until then, it's every ranita for herself.

That said, while I can't *offer* help, I sure could use some. I open my contacts and call my best friend, Sid.

"Hey, Ronnie Anne. You're up early. What's up?"

"Sid, I need help." There's a click, then dead air. "Sid?" She hung up on me! I don't even have a minute to figure out why, before someone is knocking on my bedroom door. "Who is it?" I shout. "I'm trying to make a phone call here!"

"It's me, Ronnie Anne."

"Sid?"

"I came as soon as you said you needed help."

I open the door to find my best friend standing there with a giant smile on her face. Sid was my first friend in Great Lakes City. She moved into the apartment building shortly after I did, and I could not ask for a better neighbor. Especially on mornings like this, when I'm in crisis mode.

I tell Sid everything. About the missing cake, how I was on guard duty, and how amazing La Tormenta's match was last night. Thankfully, Sid is there to keep me on track.

"So, you think someone from your family ate it?"

"It would have to be one of them, right? Or they at least snuck it away to eat later."

Sid taps her chin. "Hmm . . . Well, I can think of one way to find out."

★ ★ ★

In the basement of our apartment building, behind a hole in the laundry room wall, is a hidden room. Especially with so much family around, it's sometimes the only place to get peace and quiet. Well, peace and quiet and spiders. It's also an excellent place to hide away from your abuela when you need to run an investigation.

It's maybe not the best use of our time, but Sid and I paint the room black and white. Then we take a broken door, place it over the hole, and write SID CHANG AND RONNIE ANNE SANTIAGO, PRIVATE INVESTIGATORS on it in permanent marker.

While Sid goes to grab our first suspect, I set up a desk made out of cardboard boxes. Then I toss on a trench coat and fedora and get into character.

Finally, the suspect enters the room, all

feathers and no chill. My roommate, family pet, and regular nuisance: Sergio.

"Hey, I was promised there would be fancy crackers," he squawks. Of course his mind would be on food—he's our number-one suspect in the case of the missing tres leches. I take a toothpick and place it between my teeth, then let him sit in silence for a minute.

"Answer our questions, and we'll see about the crackers," I say slowly.

"You think I ate your cake?" he says. And just like that, I've got him!

"Funny, I don't remember asking you about cake," I respond triumphantly, taking the toothpick out of my mouth and pointing it at him.

"Well, yeah—Sid told me on the way down," Sergio says.

I glance over at Sid, who frowns. "Sorry, Ronnie Anne. I forgot that part was secret."

"Doesn't matter," Sergio continues, preening his feathers. "I went to sleep early last night and only just now woke up."

"Uh-huh. A likely story," I say. I'm not buying it. Even if Sergio didn't eat the cake, he likes to stay up late and party with Sancho, his pigeon friend. Turning in early? Yeah, right.

"Story? It is the truth!" Sergio protests.

"Oh, so we're talking truths, huh? Then you wouldn't mind if I told Abuela about that new credit card you opened in her name?"

"*Acckkk*," Sergio says, and then quickly tries to cover his beak. "I do not know . . . what you are talking about."

"Sid, do we believe Sergio?" I ask.

"Not one bit," Sid replies. Best friends always have your back.

"Fine, fine," Sergio confesses. "You're right, I went looking for the cake last night. But it was gone by the time I got there! It's not fair. Abuela never lets me have tres leches anymore." He's honest now—honest and cakeless. So we are back to square one.

"Get him out of here," I say, turning my back.

"But what about my crackers?" Sergio calls as Sid pulls him out the door. "WHAT ABOUT MY CRACKERS?!"

Next, Sid brings in my abuelo. "I like what you've done with the place," he says. "Real moody."

"Yeah, yeah," I respond. "If I were fishing for compliments, I'd head to the lake. Tell me what you did last night after Lucha."

"Well, I'm not really sure what I did right after, since I fell asleep before it was over. But when I woke up, it was dark out, and everyone had gone to bed. So I figured I would tuck in, too."

Caught him! "You went straight to bed? Without a snack?" I say.

"Oh, I had a snack," he says. I let a smile crack my facade. My dear, sweet abuelo. So carefree, so careless.

"So you had the tres leches!" I declare.

"Tres leches? Oh no, I heated up some flautas. Don't get me wrong—if the cake was in there, I would have snacked on it! Sure, I would have to deal with Abuela's chancla tomorrow, but a taste of that tres leches would have been worth it," Abuelo says, wiping drool from his mouth. With that, we are down two suspects.

The next two suspects go by quickly. Mom was working late last night. When I try to ask follow-up questions, she asks if I like having a roof over my head.

Bobby tries pulling a fast one on us and says he spent the evening video chatting with his long-distance girlfriend, Lori. But before I can even challenge him, he cracks under pressure. "Okay, I was working on my secret price-tag dance routine!" he shouts. Honestly, that tracks.

"In your apartment, that just leaves your grandmother," Sid says, sitting on the desk.

"Yep, and she does not need to know the tres leches is missing."

"So, if it's no one in your apartment, could it be one of your other family members? They were over there watching Lucha, right?" Sid asks. I nod. But I think we've wasted enough time dragging my family down here one by one. It's time we take this detective work on the road.

MY TÍO AND HIS FAMILY live in the apartment across the hall from me. On most days, both of our doors are open, and it is almost as if we have one jumbo apartment. However, when Sid and I enter, I close the door behind us. I don't want Abuela getting wise to our plan.

The first person we see is Tía Frida, poking around the living room. Seems we aren't the only people searching for something this morning.

"Morning, Tía," I say with a smile. "Weird question, but . . . can you tell us where you were last evening?"

"Morning, Ronnie Anne. Morning, Sid," Tía Frida says, distracted. "Last evening? Well, I was painting portraits of Abuela for my upcoming exhibition." I look around Frida's living room and don't see any paintings, only easels.

"These paintings . . . Where might they be?" I ask, hoping to catch her in a lie.

"Well, that is just it," Frida says, tears pooling in her eyes. "I woke up this morning, and they were missing!"

The tears are pretty convincing, and if

they're genuine, I don't want to bully her further. "Tía, I'm sorry to hear about your paintings—but it is a bit suspicious that the proof of your alibi is missing," I say, hoping we have finally found the culprit.

"I promise you, I was working on them. If you don't believe me, I can grab Abuela and she'll tell you. She was the subject of my paintings!"

Gulp! That's the last thing I want! "You know, Tía, I trust you," I say. "And, uh, good luck with finding your paintings!"

Tía points us in the direction of Tío Carlos, who is lying in his bed, staring at the ceiling. Tío Carlos is a talker, so if he did take the cake, I know he'll reveal it if we just let him ramble long enough. I ask him about last night, and he gets rolling.

"Well, last night, I had to lie down pretty early. The kids did a number on my back. But I ought to thank them—from my bed, I get a great view of the architecture of my room. Normally, I lie down and go straight to sleep, but last night, I started considering the origins of wallpaper, and—"

"Let me stop you right there, Tío," I cut him off. I need him to ramble, not lecture. "Did you, or anyone in your family, eat the tres leches cake?"

"The cake? Not that I know of. But let me tell you a fascinating history lesson about the tres leches cake . . ."

"Thanks, gotta go!" I say, and Sid and

I dash out of the room before he can get started.

I turn to Sid. "This is taking too long, and I still have all my primos to question," I say.

"Maybe we drop all the small talk and get right to the point—put them in the hot seat!"

"I'm willing to try it," I say, walking to Carlota's door. I knock and call out to her, "Hey, Carlota!"

"Hey, prima!" Carlota calls back. "Come on in."

Carlota is setting out outfits on her bed. Judging from her tripod setup, I'm guessing she has a video stream soon. Good—maybe that means she'll be distracted and she'll answer our questions quickly. Sid gives me a nudge.

"Carlota, did you eat the cake last night?" I ask.

"I did! It was simply amazing," Carlota replies, without turning from her clothes. Sid was right! Being direct works! Then Carlota keeps talking. "Well, if I'm honest, I ate quite a few different cakes. They had this amazing triple-chocolate coffee cake, and a birthday crunch cake with little teddy bear graham crackers, and then—"

"Wait, wait, wait, Carlota," Sid interrupts. "Did you eat the tres leches cake your abuela and Ronnie Anne made?"

"What? Oh, no, these cakes were from the new bakery I visited with my friends.

It's the talk of the city—they have all these wild flavors. I'll have to take you girls sometime!"

Sid and I both sigh. As much as we would both rather be at a trendy bakery, we still have to get to the bottom of this mystery.

"Thanks, Carlota. Maybe later," I say in a sulk, and we leave her room.

Next on our list is Carl and CJ, who are hanging out in their room.

"Hey, Carl. Hey, CJ," Sid says.

"We're not talking," Carl says, crossing his arms.

"Yeah, we're not saying a thing," CJ echoes.

"Oh?" Sid and I say in unison. These two just quickly shot up on my suspect list.

Carl continues, "Yeah, we know you two are going door-to-door asking what everyone did last night. And we just want to tell you that we don't know who broke my mom's portraits because they were practicing Lucha moves after they were supposed to be asleep."

So these two are probably not our cake thieves, but they sure are guilty.

"Actually, Carl," Sid responds, "we were asking about the tres leches cake."

"What's all this about Tía Frida's paintings?" I ask.

"Uh, nothing," CJ says, trying to cover. Just then, there is wailing from the living room.

"My paintings!" Tía Frida cries.

"We were never here!" Carl shouts, then pushes Sid and me out of the bedroom.

Sid shakes her head. "Another dead end."

"Yeah, and they're dead when Frida finds out they're responsible for the paintings," I say.

Sid laughs. "Good one, Ronnie Anne! Okay, so if it is not CJ or Carl, who could it be?"

"Well, I've got one cousin left, but he's not the talkative type."

A few minutes later, I'm in a staring contest with Carlitos. My baby primo is sitting on top of the dog, Lalo. With the added height, we are actually eye to eye. "Did you do it, Carlitos? Did you take my tres leches cake?" I ask, unblinking. Carlitos tilts his head. I tilt mine to match. After a minute, I can feel my eyelids twitching. Finally, I cave and blink. Carlitos laughs.

"I don't speak baby," Sid says. "Did he take the cake?"

"I wish I could tell you, but there is no cracking him. That said, there isn't a crumb on him, and if he ate the cake, he would have a mess to match. I don't think he's our thief."

A few minutes later, Sid and I sit in the apartment building's stairwell. "Well, that was a complete waste of a morning," I grumble.

"I'm not sure," Sid says. "We did get a recommendation for a new bakery!" She laughs, and I can't help but join her. Even though I'm in a sour mood, she has my back 100 percent.

"Excuse me, girls," comes a voice from down the stairs. It's Mr. Nakamura, one of my upstairs neighbors. Sid and I scoot to the side, and he passes us.

That seems to give Sid an idea. "You know, Ronnie Anne, maybe it wasn't your family who took the cake. Maybe it was someone else in the building."

"You really think it could be?"

"The way you and your abuela talk up that recipe? Absolutely! But it won't be as easy questioning them. Carl and CJ were onto us. We need to be more clever. We need a plan."

5

SID AND I STAND next to her fridge, its door closed. "You know, Sid, I trust you. I know you didn't take the cake," I say.

"Well, of course I didn't, Ronnie Anne, but can I really trust my family? This is the only way that clears us."

Sid grabs the handle and closes her eyes. Then she opens the door.

"Whew!" Sid lets out a sigh of relief. "No cakes."

"You two looking for a snack?" It's Becca, Sid's mom.

"No," Sid responds, "we're looking for a missing cake. I just had to make sure you, Dad, or Adelaide didn't take it."

"Well, I don't know how I feel about you thinking we are a family of crooks, but even so, we've been busy all morning building the pen on the roof for the party," Becca says.

"Pen?" I ask.

"For the exotic petting zoo!" Sid's mom works at the zoo. Almost every weekend, there's a new animal that she's rehabbing at their apartment. "Anyhow, I need to head back upstairs. And remember, Sid, you promised you would help. After we're finished with the pen, we'll need help bathing the baby kangaroos!"

"I know, Mom. Let me just do a bit more digging for Ronnie Anne."

"Sounds good," Becca says. "See you two later."

Sid turns to me. "Well, that clears apartment 3A. Who's next?" she asks.

"Probably Mrs. Flores and Alexis. But we can't just go into each of our neighbors' apartments asking to see inside their fridges."

"Right." Sid thinks for a moment. "And there's certainly no chance they'll let us in if they're the ones who stole it."

Hmmm. We both ponder for a few minutes.

Then it hits me. "I've got a plan!"

* * *

"You ready?" Sid asks. I nod, and then I start dancing, hopping from one foot to the other and holding my shoulders up to my ears.

"How do I look?"

"Perfect!" Sid says, and knocks on the door to Mrs. Flores's apartment. A moment later, her son, Alexis, opens the door.

"Hey there, Sid, Ronnie Anne!"

"H-hey, Alexis," I stammer. "Can I use your bathroom? Sergio was using our toi-let as a personal spa—"

"It even has whirlpool action," Sid chimes in.

"Right," I continue, "he got a lot of his feathers stuck in it, and it's plugged up. My abuela is fixing it right now. But I had a lot of orange juice with breakfast and—"

"Go on! Go on!" Alexis says, stepping aside. I dash inside, toward the bathroom at first, and I hear Sid pick up the conversation.

"So, are you coming to the party tonight?" she asks Alexis.

"You know it! I'm even practicing a new song on my tuba to perform!"

Once I know he's distracted, I sneak into the kitchen and quietly open the fridge door. There's no tres leches. Honestly, it's a relief to know that my neighbors aren't sneaking around and stealing cakes. I make my way to the bathroom, then flush. Moments later, Sid and I are waving goodbye to Alexis.

"Any cake?" Sid asks once the door is closed.

"Nope," I say. "Let's keep going!"

I tell the same lie about Sergio to each of our neighbors. I'm in and out of Mr. Nakamura's apartment in no time, but not before he has Nelson, his dog, demonstrate one of the tricks he plans to show off at the party. Mrs. Kernicky isn't home— she's probably at her yoga class. Plus, she's always so busy staying fit that I really doubt she would make time to steal a cake.

The last apartment on the fourth floor is occupied by Miranda and Georgia. Once inside, I actually do have to use the bathroom. But when I finish with that, I take a peek in the fridge—still no sign of the tres leches.

"What took you so long?" Sid asks once I'm back. "They had me carrying up beanbags to the roof for a cornhole tournament!"

"Sorry," I say, defeated. "No cake here, either. Is that it, then? Do we just give up?"

"Not yet, Ronnie Anne," Sid says, trying to lift my spirits. "I do have one last thought, but it's a messy one."

"Let me hear it."

"So far, we have been assuming that if a

neighbor took it, they were just hiding the cake. But maybe they ate it and have already thrown away the evidence."

"I was thinking about that, and I made a point to check everyone's trash, too!" I say.

"I was thinking bigger, Ronnie Anne."

Oh no.

6

I'M HALFWAY DOWN THE INSIDE of the dumpster and feeling glad I decided to have lunch *after* our deep dumpster diving. The hazmat suits Sid and I made from raincoats, trash bags, goggles, and lots of duct tape keep the gross out. But even if I can't smell the trash surrounding me, being this close to yesterday's food scraps still makes me queasy. And if I toss my cookies, I'm worried my suit would work just as well keeping puke in as it does keeping trash out.

"Hey there, Ronnie Anne," Sid says, poking her head between a few trash bags, "you okay?"

"Yeah, I'll be all right. No signs of cake pans yet, though," I say, closing one bag and moving to the next. "How about you?"

"Nothing yet." Sid grabs another bag, and there's something about it that looks familiar . . .

"Sid, look out! That's one of the special deodorizing bags we use for Carlitos's diapers!" I cry.

I push off the side of the dumpster, propelling myself toward Sid, and grab her just before the packed bag of diapers explodes. We sink backward, farther into the dumpster.

"Thanks, Ronnie Anne," Sid says. "You saved me from a diaper disaster!" I can hear her, but I can't see her. This far down, sunlight no longer pours in from above. But strangely, there seem to be some lights coming from below.

What could those be? I dive even deeper into the dumpster. After pushing past a few bags and then suddenly dropping down a few feet, I find myself in a cavity at the bottom of the dumpster. For some reason, there are Christmas lights strung up and blazing. "What in the—"

"Well, excuse you!" It's Sergio, sitting

at a makeshift table made out of trash. Next to him is Sancho, his busted pigeon friend.

A moment later, Sid crashes down on top of me.

"*OOF!*" I cry.

"Sorry, Ronnie Anne. Wait, where are we?"

"In our exclusive restaurant!" Sergio squawks. Sure enough, he and Sancho have little plates of last week's thrown-away leftovers in front of them.

"Ew, you're going to eat that?" I ask.

"Hey now, I don't come to your trash buffet and judge your food, do I?" Sergio retorts.

"Sergio," Sid butts in, trying to keep the

peace. "That looks . . . appetizing. Any chance you found any tres leches for dessert?"

"I wish!" Sergio replies. "It would be the perfect addition to our four-course meal. Trust me—if there was a hint of tres leches in this dumpster, I'd be celebrating for weeks!"

"Good to know, Sergio," Sid says.

"Now, if you'll excuse us, our brunch is getting stale!"

Sid and I nod to each other before leaping out of the trash cavity and back into the dumpster above. A minute later, we've climbed our way to the top of the trash.

"Well, we can be sure the tres leches wasn't tossed," Sid says, taking off her hazmat suit and leaving it on top of the rest of the trash.

"Yeah," I say, tossing my suit on top of hers as we climb out of the dumpster. "But then where did it go? No one in my family took it, and neither did the neighbors. A cake doesn't just disappear! Unless maybe it was a race of cake-eating aliens that came to devour it?"

"Ronnie Anne . . ."

"You're right, Sid. It was most likely a swarm of sewer rats."

"Ronnie Anne, I think it's time you tell your abuela," Sid says. "Come clean that you didn't keep a close eye on it. Maybe the two of you can bake another one before tonight, while there's still time."

"Sid, you're a genius!"

"Wow, Ronnie Anne, I'm glad you agree. I was worried you wouldn't want to tell her," Sid says.

"Oh, not about that. I'm definitely not telling her," I reply. "But I can make a replacement cake! That way, she'll never have to know it was gone!"

Sid is right that there isn't a lot of time left. And while it's ideal for a tres leches cake to soak overnight, I figure that if I can have it soaking for a few hours, that should be enough. "We should still have all the ingredients in the kitchen. You and I can make it in no time!"

"All right, Ronnie Anne, let's do it!" Sid says. It's been a stressful morning, to say the least, but with Sid by my side, I know I can handle whatever comes next. Then Sid's phone rings. "It's my mom. Give me a minute. Hey, Mom, what's up?"

As Sid talks to her mom, I remember that I still haven't gotten back to my dad about what to bring to the party. However, I have to stay on task. I should be able to make another cake in an hour or so. If I call him after that, it should still give him enough time to bring something last-minute.

"Bad news, Ronnie Anne," Sid says after ending her call. "My mom needs help setting up the petting zoo pen on the roof now. Are you going to be okay making the cake without me?"

I think for a minute. I could make the

cake on my own, but the longer I'm in the kitchen, the more likely Abuela will catch me. I'm going to need some help.

Suddenly, I hear someone crying loudly from near the front doors of the apartment building. Sid and I turn to see Tía Frida, carrying her destroyed paintings to the dumpster.

"Hey, Tía," I say. "Looks like you found your paintings. Do you know what happened to them?" My question starts her wailing all over again.

"I"—*sob*—"found them"—*sob*—"behind the couch." If you haven't caught on, Tía Frida is very in touch with her emotions. At first, I worried about her, but I've come to learn that it drives her art.

Her art . . . that gives me an idea.

"I'm so sorry, Tía," I say. "But why not do a new series of paintings now? One that, uh, captures the sorrow of lost art? Maybe Abuela would be willing to model again?" Tía Frida's wails turn to sniffles.

"You know, Ronnie Anne, that's not a bad idea."

"It's a great idea! And you should start right now, and take around an hour or so of Abuela's time!" I reply.

Sid snickers. She can tell what I'm up to.

"I will! And maybe I can even give a preview of it this evening at the party!" With that, Tía Frida dashes back inside.

"Well done, Ronnie Anne!" Sid says.

"You bought yourself some time in the kitchen. Sorry again that I can't help you out."

"You've already been a great help today, Sid," I say. "And I know just who I can get to help me bake . . ."

7

"TELL ME AGAIN why we have to help you?" Carl asks as he mixes the wet ingredients in a metal bowl. He's stirring so quickly that the egg-and-milk mixture starts to splash out of the bowl.

"Because if you don't, I'm telling your mother that you destroyed her paintings," I reply, pulling Abuela's recipe card away from flying ingredients. "And slow down, will you?!"

I look back at the recipe and read the next line aloud. "Okay, CJ, we need one and three-fourths cups of flour." CJ takes the measuring cup and scoops the flour before leveling it off.

"One cup of flour!" CJ says, then pours it into a bowl of dry ingredients and grabs the one-fourth cup to measure the rest. Aside from Carl's erratic stirring, things are going pretty well. At this pace, we'll have a second cake in the oven in no time. I can't believe I didn't think of this sooner!

There is one small problem, however. The recipe calls for a quarter teaspoon of the "secret ingredient." Even though I know it adds a spicy flavor, and that it would otherwise be unusual for a cake, I have no idea what it is. I was hoping Abuela would have noted down the ingredient on the recipe, but it looks like it's a secret she keeps locked away. Of course, she did try to share it with me. *Ugh!* I curse myself for not paying closer attention.

"What's next, Ronnie Anne?" CJ asks. I give him the remaining list of dry ingredients. Since I don't know what gives it the same kick, I'll have to make my best guess.

I open the cabinet that Abuela reached into for the ingredient and look around. Hmm. The recipe already has cinnamon in it. I see garlic powder, cumin, oregano . . .

none of those seem right. There's tabasco sauce, chili peppers, cayenne, and lots of other ground-up spices with hard-to-read labels. Which one of those would make tres leches spicy and also better? I close my eyes and reach in, pulling out the hot sauce. Here goes nothing.

"Okay, CJ, we need one-fourth teaspoon of this hot sauce. Add it to Carl's bowl."

Once we've mixed both the wet and dry ingredients, we each dip our fingers in and try the batter. It's sweet, but it's missing the kick from before.

"Maybe it wasn't the hot sauce," I say.

"Or maybe we need more!" Carl says, grabbing the bottle and pouring it straight in.

"Carl!" I exclaim, snatching the bottle back. The hot sauce pools red on top of the batter. It definitely doesn't look right. "Well . . . might as well stir it in."

While CJ and Carl finish the batter, I check the recipe card for how to make the tres leches mix. Right! I need three kinds of milk: condensed, evaporated, and heavy cream. Once again, I open the cabinets—and realize we have a problem. "We don't have any more evaporated milk!"

"No one wants a dos leches cake," CJ jokes. Carl laughs, but I don't have time to respond.

"I'm heading down to the Mercado to see if they have any evaporated milk.

You two finish making the batter!"

"Can we at least have a taste first?" Carl pleads.

"Fine! But just a taste, to make sure it's got the spicy kick! And it better be a small taste. Promise?"

"We promise," my primos say in unison. In seconds, I'm out the door and running down to the store. I'm not sure I trust them completely, but as long as I'm back upstairs quickly, what's the worst that could happen?

8

THE MERCADO is on the ground level of the apartment building. My abuelo runs it, but Bobby works there now, too. It's a small shop, but it always has just what you need. It's incredibly convenient to live above a grocery store, especially if you get a family discount.

I head into the Mercado and give a wave

to my brother behind the counter. "Hey, Bobby."

"Hey, Ronnie Anne, what brings you in?"

"Need some more evaporated milk."

"Check the second aisle!" he calls out before burying his head in some papers behind the counter. I'm not sure what he's working on, but I imagine it's something business-y. Ever since moving to Great Lakes City, Bobby has put his all into running the Mercado.

It doesn't take me long to find the evaporated milk, and thankfully I got the last can. But . . .

"Hey, Bobby, there's no price on this!"

"Good observation, Ronnie Anne," he says, coming down the aisle, his trusty price tag sticker gun in hand. I look up and down the aisle and realize NONE of the items have prices on them.

"Are you slacking off?" I ask.

"I need you to film me."

"Huh? Bobby, I don't have time for whatever it is you're up to!"

"Please, Ronnie Anne—I'll pay for the milk if you do!"

"Fine." I give in. I'll waste more time if I argue. "So what is it you need me to film, and what does this have to do with the missing price tags?"

Bobby holds up the piece of paper he was just working on. "First, I made a map of all the items in the Mercado. Then I memorized the exact prices of each item."

"Okay . . . ?"

"And I've developed a dance routine to take me around the store and price every item. I've been trying to figure out how I can record it to show at the party tonight. And to send to Lori—you know we have a special anniversary tonight."

"Bobby, if you stop talking about Lori and start dancing, I'll split the price of the evaporated milk with you." I cannot waste any more time.

"Sounds good," Bobby says, passing me his phone. "Now I just need to set the mood." He walks to the back of the store and kicks open all the coolers. An icy fog rolls out into the aisles. Then he flips two switches. The first turns off the lights, the second kicks on lasers, which bounce around the store. I have to admit, it's pretty impressive.

"All right, it starts up here," Bobby says, and he ducks below the counter. I click RECORD. From behind the counter, Bobby turns on some music. I don't recognize the song, but it's got a very catchy beat, and I can't help but start to dance along.

Bobby leaps onto the counter and does a spin, tagging a few counter treats with his sticker gun. He flips off the counter and shimmies down the aisle. And then he starts singing!

"Bubble gum, half a dollar—two thirteen for a melon baller . . ."

Soon, he's made his way to the coolers. The fog catches the lasers, and for a minute, I forget I'm in the Mercado and feel like I'm at a concert. "Go, Bobby!" I shout before remembering I'm recording. He goes door-to-door, spinning, labeling every last item, and closing the cooler doors behind him.

Finally, Bobby busts a move down the last aisle, tagging mangoes, bananas, and oranges. He finishes with a flourish, pointing his sticker gun in the air. A shower of price stickers falls like confetti around him, and the music hits its peak.

"Bravo! Bravo!" I shout, and hand him back his phone.

"Thanks, Ronnie Anne. And here's that can of evaporated milk."

He hands me the can, and I eye the sticker.

"Twenty-two dollars?! Even half off, that's a bad deal!"

"Wait, twenty-two dollars? That can't be right! Evaporated milk is two sixty-five." Bobby starts frantically picking up items off the shelves. "Oh no! I must have miscounted. Every sticker is off by one! Any chance you can give me a hand?"

But I'm out the door before I can answer.

★ ★ ★

As soon as I enter our kitchen, I drop the can of evaporated milk. It hits the floor and rolls until it stops at CJ's feet. CJ and Carl sit on the floor, their backs against the cabinets and their bellies poking out from under their shirts. All around them are traces of cake batter. In between them is the empty batter bowl.

"What did you do?!" I yell, even though I know the answer. They both groan in response.

After a moment, Carl manages a few words. "We just had a small taste while we waited. We didn't think it was spicy enough, so we added more hot sauce. Then we had another small taste after that."

"And another small taste after that," CJ adds.

"Please tell me some of the batter made it into the oven." I know it's a long shot, and they both shake their head no.

"Maybe it's a good thing, Ronnie Anne," CJ says in between groans. "I've tasted Abuela's tres leches batter before, and I don't think the hot sauce was the secret ingredient."

Maybe he's right. As mad as I am, this cake would never have passed Abuela's taste test.

"Ronnie Anne," Carl says, "are you going to tell our mom about the paintings?"

I look at the pair of them, stuffed full

of raw cake batter and sweating from the amount of hot sauce they ingested. This seems like punishment enough.

"No, your secret is safe with me. But you *will* need to clean this up."

"Thanks, Ronnie Anne," Carl says before passing out in the bowl face-first.

I go back to my room and fall onto my bed. I'm still without a cake. And with only a few hours before the party, I'm completely out of ideas. I can't find the tres leches. I can't make a tres leches. Suddenly, I sit straight up: "I can buy a tres leches!"

q

"AND THAT'S IT FOR today's summer
looks! Thanks for watching, and—
RONNIE ANNE!"

Oops. I back out of the doorway and
close the door to Carlota's room after
making a brief cameo in her latest post. If
I want to know the deets about her bakery, I definitely don't want to be on her
bad side.

A minute later, Carlota opens the door and stares me down.

"Sorry, Carlota, I'll knock next time," I say through a big grin.

Carlota sighs and lets me in. "It's fine—and honestly, viewers enjoy a little bit of chaos. If I'm lucky, your guilty face will go viral." Carlota sits on her bed and gestures for me to join her. "What's up, prima?"

I lay it all out for her: the missing tres leches, the botched baking attempt, and my newest need.

"That new trendy bakery, the one you visited with your friends—do you think it has tres leches?"

"Let me check." She pulls out her phone

and starts tapping on the screen. "Looks like it's your lucky day, Ronnie Anne. They have a Triple Leches."

"Triple?"

Carlota shrugs. "I'm sure it's the same. They're just trying to give it a trendy name."

"Good enough!" I grab Carlota's arm and drag her out the door. "You've gotta take me right away!"

★ ★ ★

Carlota leads me to a GLART station a few blocks away. "We just need to take the train four stops, and voilà, we will have your cake in no time!" As we head down the steps underground, my phone starts ringing. "Who's calling you?"

"It's my dad. He's been trying to contact me all day about what he can bring to the party."

I answer the video call, but as Carlota and I go farther into the station, the audio starts cutting out. "Be quick—the train is almost here," Carlota says as we reach the platform.

"Hola—Ranita . . . ideas," my dad's staticky face says. Then the call disconnects. I quickly open up my texts and shoot off a quick response: *Can't talk. Need tres leches.*

The guilt about not helping out my dad is starting to build, but I have to stay focused.

Soon, Carlota and I are off the train and

exiting the station. We come out right in front of Cutest Cakes Bakeshop. "Here we are!" Carlota says. "Let's take a quick selfie in front of the store. Ronnie Anne?"

I can't contain my excitement—I've already rushed into the store. I should have come up with this idea hours ago! I make a beeline for the counter, and one of the bakers greets me with a smile.

"Well, hello there! You look ready for one of our cutest cakes!"

"I am! Do you have one of the tres leches—er, I mean, tres milks, or—"

The baker cuts me off. "Triple leches? Right over here." He walks along the back side of the display case, and as I look at all the options, my stomach starts to sink.

There are lots of cakes on display, but they're all round and very small. "Would you like one or a dozen?"

"Are these all cupcakes?" I ask, my heart and my hope dropping further and further.

"Not cupcakes—cutest cakes!" Carlota says from right behind me.

I manage to whimper, "Cutest cakes?!" before sliding down the display and ending up face-first on the floor. Without looking up, I ask the baker, "You don't happen to make any full-size cakes, do you?"

"Nope, only our trademark *cutest cakes*."

Carlota tries to help. "Ronnie Anne, you could always get a dozen and try to squish them together." I roll over and stare at my prima. "Yeah . . . that won't fool Abuela."

This is it. I'm done. I'm going to return home with a tray of "cutest" cakes, and Abuela will kick me out of the family. I start to roll my way to the door. Who cares how filthy and covered in crumbs the floor is? I deserve this fate.

"You could always try the panadería next store," the baker offers.

"The what?!" I sit up so fast I slam my head on a table. "Ow." After my vision returns, I ask again, "Are you telling me there is a Mexican bakery next door?" I turn to look at Carlota. "And you took me to Cutest Cakes?"

Carlota shrugs. "You said you wanted to go to the trendy new place . . ."

I shout a quick "thank you" and bolt outside. Sure enough, right next door is a small shop with a weathered sign above it: PANADERÍA, PASTELES PARA TODA OCASIÓN.

I open the door and am greeted by the sweet smells of pastries. The store is pretty bare, but lining the walls are various display cases and coolers. *I'm here for the cake*, I remind myself, but it doesn't hurt to see what pastries they have in stock. This late in the afternoon, the cases are mostly picked over. However, a few fluffy conchas, pink and brown, are sitting on blue trays inside the cases. Below those are golden-brown and crispy orejas, just waiting to be eaten. I use my sleeve to wipe some drool from my mouth.

"Hola, niña," says an older man from behind the counter. "¿Cuál le gusta?"

"Hola, do you have any tres leches?"

He nods and points to a cooler in the corner. I run and press my face to the glass. Right there, on the bottom shelf, is a tres leches cake. It is adorned with whipped cream, strawberries, and cinnamon—just like Abuela's. It's such a beautiful sight, I start crying, and my tears freeze my cheek to the cooler door. Whoops!

"You found it!" Carlota says.

"Uh-huh," I say, trying to free my face. She grabs my head and pulls, and I come loose, swinging the cooler door open. Open to my majestic tres leches.

I bring the cake to the counter and pull out my wallet. "How much for the cake, señor?" Just then, I hear Carlota's stomach growl from across the panadería. I catch her eyeing the conchas.

I revise my question. "How much for the cake and two conchas?"

Five minutes later, Carlota and I sit on the GLART with the tres leches secure between us and a concha each. For the first time all day, I start to relax. Sure, the cake only looks like Abuela's—I still have to figure out what to do about the taste. But the hard part is over.

10

"SO, ARE YOU BRINGING it to the roof in that?" Carlota asks as we stand outside the apartment building. I look at the cake in my hands and see the problem. The cake is in a lined cardboard box. If I bring this to the roof, I might as well be putting a price sticker on top of it. Even if it's from a real panadería, it still is store-bought.

"Carlota, I appreciate you bringing this up, but couldn't you have thought of this on the train?" I grumble. So much for being relaxed.

"I'm sure you'll figure it out, prima," Carlota says, heading inside. "Now if you'll excuse me, I have to get ready for the party."

"Carlota, wait—"

"Thanks for the concha!" The door slams.

"Okay, this is fine. I just need to get this into the kitchen, into one of Abuela's pans, and onto the roof without her seeing me. Piece of—"

"Cake!"

I'm so startled I toss the tres leches into

the air, but manage to grab it again. Once it's secure in my hands, I turn and see Sergio behind me. "Sergio! Are you kidding me?!"

"So, you found your missing tres leches," he says, his eyes going wide. He licks his lips. "Although . . . that doesn't look like Abuela's cake."

"It's not," I say with a huff. "Now, if you'll excuse me, I need to find a way to sneak this cake inside."

"If you're looking for help, Ronnie Anne, I'm your bird."

I look into his cake-starved eyes. "Go on . . ."

"I just need to flip a few breakers here, spend a few credit card points there, and

I'll have Abuela chasing me around the building, giving you the cover to get in and get out."

"And what's in it for you?"

"Why, only the first slice of cake," Sergio says, putting on a sad puppy-parrot face. "Abuela no longer lets me eat her tres leches because she says it rots my beak." I recall Abuela saying something about Sergio and her cake last night—some sort of "incident"—but I don't think she told me any other details. Sergio holds out a wing. "Deal?"

I set down the cake and shake it. "Deal."

★ ★ ★

I hide around the bottom of the apartment stairwell, listening for my cue. It feels like

I'm waiting for an eternity, and what was a refrigerator-cold cake is starting to warm up.

Suddenly, I hear Abuela holler, "YOU DID WHAT?!" and a second later, I hear our apartment door slam open. There's a frantic flapping of wings and the terrifyingly quick tap of Abuela's shoes as she chases Sergio farther upstairs.

I run, careful to keep the cake in balance. Within seconds, I'm inside the apartment, and I close and lock the door behind me. I have no time to spare—I hear Sergio and Abuela whiz back down the hall and down the stairs. Soon, I'm in the kitchen. I set the cake down and grab a pan. Even with Abuela out of the apartment, I still have one challenge left: I need to squeeze this cake into that pan without losing any of the tres leches goodness. I tear off the top of the box and hold it just above the pan. Sweat pools on my forehead. The kitchen goes silent except for the beating of my heart.

One. Two. Tres. Leches.

I push my arm upward, sending the cake flying toward the ceiling. Then I fling the cake box out the window, grab the pan, and . . .

PLOP! The cake lands in the pan perfectly, splashing some of the tres leches up and over the edges and onto my face.

It's delicious. I clean up the mess, then cover the cake in plastic wrap and grab paper plates, a serving knife, and forks. Everything in hand, I make my way up to the roof, just in time for the start of the party.

II

AS I SET the tres leches on the table, it's like a weight has been lifted. Even though the sun has started to set, I can feel its warmth, and even the air feels clearer. Everything is good. I lay out the plates, forks, and cake knife. Then, I walk away, find a lawn chair, and take a seat. I did it!

The party is about to start and most of the guests are already here. Miranda and

Georgia have set up the two boards for playing cornhole, each complete with a stack of beanbags. Alexis is polishing his tuba. I'm used to hearing that thing echo through the hallway, and I imagine it has to sound better up here. One whole corner of the roof has been dedicated to the pop-up petting zoo. Sid and her mother tend to the animals. From my vantage point, I see a few kangaroos, and—is that a koala? I have to make sure I pet that koala tonight.

I take a deep, satisfied breath. Tonight, I get to pet a koala and eat a slice of tres leches. Sweet, cinnamony, spicy—*GASP!* The spice!

I'd gotten so excited about having a cake to bring, I forgot that we were going to eat it! If Abuela has so much as one taste . . .

Then I have a thought: Abuela doesn't necessarily need to have a slice.

I jump out of my seat and do a quick head count of the party. I need to cut and serve this cake as fast as possible. Abuela won't be too sad if she doesn't get a slice, as long as people tell her how delicious it is. Soon, I have the cake cut into fifteen pieces. But as I wait for the guests to line up for it, no one does. So I take matters, and two slices of cake, into my own hands.

"Hey, Miranda. Hey, Georgia," I say, approaching with two plates of tres leches. "Want some cake?"

"Oh," Georgia says. "Well, I was going to save mine for later . . ."

"I'll take mine now!" Miranda says, and reaches for the plate.

"RONNIE ANNE!" I turn and see Sergio flying a mile a minute across the roof. Oh, right! I promised him the first piece.

"Sergio, chill," I say. "There's more on the table."

But he doesn't hear me. Instead, he opens his beak so wide he seems to unhinge his jaw, eating Miranda's slice—and the plate and fork—in one bite.

"Sergio!" I scold him, but he still isn't listening. Instead, his eyes start blinking quickly. Then his feathers twitch. He begins whispering something, but I can't hear him. I lean in and start to make it out.

"Tres leches. Tres. Leches. TRES LECHES!!"

Oh no, I think. *The incident.*

In an instant, Sergio darts straight up in the air, then pivots and dive-bombs back down. He collides with the pile of beanbags, scattering them across the roof. Miranda, Georgia, and I duck and cover, and I watch as one of the beanbags hurtles into Alexis's tuba. But Alexis didn't see it and tries to begin his performance. As he blows into his tuba, his face is getting redder and redder, but there's no sound coming out. He takes a deep breath, blows into it again, and then—*THOOF!*

The beanbag rockets out of the tuba and straight toward the petting zoo! It ping-pongs around the cage, tripping Sid, knocking over Becca, and then bashing the gate, opening it wide.

Oh no—the kangaroos! With no gate to hold them back, they start hopping with no plan of stopping. One of them makes a bee-line for the snack table. It leaps up and comes crashing down on the side of the table, cata-pulting the slices of cake into the air. It feels as if they're moving in slow motion as I try to scramble to my feet in time. The pieces of cake fly higher and higher . . . and before I know it, they're over the side of the roof and tumbling down, down, down.

"*My tres leches!*" I scream.

"MY TRES LECHES!" Sergio screams, and he flies over the edge of the building.

12

"OH NO. OH NO, OH NO, OH NO." I peer over the edge of the roof. Four stories down, I see Sergio licking the cake off the cement.

"Mija, careful near the edge of the roof," I hear from behind me. My stomach plummets down four stories as well, as I turn around to see Abuela. The rest of the roof is still in chaos as Sid and her parents try to grab the last of the loose animals. But Abuela pays them no mind.

"Sorry, Abuela," I say, stepping forward. Once I'm away from the edge, she turns to look at the food table. She lifts an eyebrow.

"Ay, mija, did you forget to grab the cake?"

The whole day flashes in front of me. The missing cake, the interrogations . . . the dumpster diving, the batter fiasco . . . Bobby's dance routine, and the panadería. I lost a perfectly good day trying to fix last night's mistake, and it was all for nothing.

I let out a long sigh. "Abuela, about the cake . . ." I begin. *Here you go, Ronnie Anne,* I think. "Last night, I skipped out on guard duty. And when I went to check this morning, your tres leches cake was gone. I spent all day trying to replace it. But I should have come and told you sooner."

I feel the weight of the day lift off my shoulders. Whatever punishment is in store for me won't be pretty, but at least the guilt is gone. I look up at Abuela, waiting for her response.

Instead of yelling or grabbing her chancla, Abuela leans back and laughs and laughs.

"Huh?" I say. Honestly, this is even scarier.

"You're right, Ronnie Anne, it was wrong for you to stop watching the cake—pero, you should also have come to talk to me sooner. Because the cake isn't missing."

"It isn't?"

"No, mija! Last night, after my portrait, I took the cake down to the Mercado. Hector always gets up for a midnight snack, so I had to make sure it wasn't in the fridge."

"You're kidding me!" I say, and I can't help but smile. I didn't lose the cake!

"Yep, it's in the cooler, all the way to the left, on the bottom rack. Now go grab it, quick, so we can get this party started!"

Abuela doesn't need to tell me twice. I sprint to the roof access door and down the stairs. I pass the fourth floor, then the third, thinking about how I snuck into each of my neighbors' apartments to inspect their fridges, when the actual cake was under my nose the whole time. I pass the second floor, then practically leap down the last flight of stairs. I open the front door and enter the Mercado.

"Hey, Bobby!" I shout as I sprint down the aisle to the coolers in the back. I open the cooler all the way to the left, and crouch down.

And there on the bottom shelf is . . . nothing!

Once again, the tres leches is missing.

13

I STARE AT THE BOTTOM SHELF until Bobby comes over and closes the door. I almost wish he would just lock me in there, so I don't have to face Abuela. How could the cake have disappeared from here?! It's not like we sell tres leches at the Mercado.

"Hey, sis, if you're just looking, do you mind closing the cooler door?" Bobby says.

"After the routine earlier, I need to make sure it stays cold in there."

I slap my hand to my forehead. "Your routine!"

"What about it?" Bobby asks, walking back to the counter.

"Can I see your phone?" I ask, following him.

"Sure thing, let me just text Lori quick—"

I grab the phone from his hand. "She can wait."

"Hey!"

I find the dance video and scrub through it, pausing when Bobby does a twirl in front of the cooler. "There!" I shout and zoom in. The image is blurry, but at the bottom of the frame is the tres leches, right where Abuela said it would be. I keep playing the video and watch as Bobby leans down, and—*BAM*—places a sticker on the cake.

"Oh, that's why my item count was off," Bobby says. "I didn't know that was there and I priced it by accident, which then messed up the prices of everything after it! So, what happened to it?"

"I was hoping you could tell me," I say, glaring at him. My brother may have the smarts to operate the Mercado, but other times I worry about him. "Do you remember selling the cake to anyone?"

"A cake? I don't remember. Honestly, I've been so caught up in my dance routine today. And then texting Lori about my dance routine." Bobby starts twirling behind the counter. "And then thinking about me and Lori dancing, and . . . What was the question, Ronnie Anne?"

"Do you know who bought the cake?"

"Oh . . . no. Sorry, Ronnie Anne. This might be a mystery that goes unsolved."

I drop my head. This really isn't Bobby's fault, as much as I want it to be. If I'd confessed to Abuela earlier today, I could have come and grabbed the cake then. "Well, bye, Bobby," I say, and leave the Mercado.

Back outside, I think about heading back up to the party cake-less, and instead sit on the stoop. Today is going down in history as one of the worst days of my life.

"Hola, Ronnie Anne! Here to greet me?"

I look up to see my dad, and quickly drop my head again. *Chihuahua!* On top of everything else, I never even got back to him.

"Hey, Dad," I mutter.

"Ranita, what's the matter?" he says, sitting down next to me.

"It's just been a long day. I was supposed to bring a tres leches cake to the party, and just when I thought everything was going to be okay, I found out Bobby sold it!"

"Wait," Dad says slowly. "You don't mean this tres leches, do you?" I tilt my head to look at him, and there in his hands is Abuela's pan—our tres leches.

"Dad! How in the world?!"

"Why are you surprised? I thought you asked me to buy it!" he says.

"I did?"

Dad pulls out his phone and shows me my text: *Can't talk. Need tres leches.*

"I thought you were asking for me to pick one up. I went to a panadería near my house first, but they had just sold the last one. Luckily, I found this at the Mercado. Only ninety-nine cents, too! Which reminds me, I need to pay Bobby for it. When I tried to the first time, he was just dancing behind the counter with his phone taped to a mop. I didn't want to disturb him. Anyway, the cake needed toppings, so I just ran home and finished decorating, which is why I'm running a bit late."

I can't even find the words to say, so I just give my dad a huge hug instead.

"Careful, Ranita! Don't make me drop the cake."

"Oh, sorry!" I say, laughing. He sets the cake down and hugs me back. "Thank you so much, Dad."

"Thank you for the idea! Now, let's get to that party already, huh?" I nod, and he hands me the cake, and together we head inside.

★ ★ ★

"Ronnie Anne, this is amazing!" Sid says, and she shovels her last bite of tres leches into her mouth.

"Mhmm," my neighbors chorus in agreement, mouths full of cake.

Sid licks her plate clean. "I would think a soggy cake wouldn't work, but it's almost like it's soaked in melted ice cream."

I take a bite of my slice. Sid's description isn't too far off. The cake almost melts in my mouth. It's incredibly sweet, with strong hints of cinnamon, vanilla, and—

Sid lets out a flaming burp. "Wow, that is some heat! What *is* that, Ronnie Anne?"

"Uh, it—it's . . ." I stammer, and Abuela comes up from behind me.

"It's a family secret," she says.

"Well, it's a tasty secret," Sid says with a grin. "I'm going to get some more and see if I can figure out what it is."

With Sid out of earshot, I lean on my abuela.

"Hey, Abuela," I say in between bites, "thanks again for forgiving me."

"Mija." Abuela wraps me in a hug. "Forgiveness is easy when you are honest."

"Can I be honest about something else?"

"Sure."

"I wasn't listening when you told me what the secret ingredient was," I say. "Sorry."

"Oh, I know. And I forgive you."

"Will you still share it with me?"

Abuela leans over and whispers, "A pinch of cayenne."

"Oh! That's much better than hot sauce!"

"Hot sauce?" Abuela says in surprise.

After a pause, she continues, "You know, if you and I tweaked a few things, I bet we could make that work."

I take another bite and recognize the hint of cayenne. Then I let out a flaming burp. "Nah, no need to fix what's perfect."

Recipe for Mamá Lupe's Tres Leches Surprise Cake

Ingredients:

For the Cake:

- 1¾ cups/225 grams all-purpose flour
- ½ cup/45 grams unsweetened Dutch-processed cocoa powder
- 1½ teaspoons baking soda
- 1½ teaspoons baking powder
- ½ teaspoon fine sea salt
- 1½ cups/300 grams granulated sugar
- 1 teaspoon ground cinnamon
- ¼ teaspoon ground cayenne pepper or chili pepper
- 2 eggs, at room temperature
- 1 cup/240 milliliters whole milk
- ½ cup/120 milliliters grapeseed oil or any mild-flavored oil
- ½ teaspoon vanilla extract
- 1 cup/240 milliliters boiling water

For the Tres Leches:

- 1 (12-ounce) can/355 milliliters evaporated milk
- 1 (14-ounce) can/395 milliliters sweetened condensed milk (3 tablespoons reserved for the whipped cream)
- 1 cup/240 milliliters heavy cream
- 1 teaspoon vanilla extract

For the Condensed Milk Whipped Cream:

- 1 cup/240 milliliters heavy cream, chilled
- ½ teaspoon vanilla extract
- 1 teaspoon cinnamon, plus more for decoration
- Sliced strawberries for decoration

Adult supervision required.

Directions:

1. Preheat the oven to 350°F. Grease the bottom only of a 9-by-13-inch cake pan (preferably metal), leaving a ¼-inch border that remains ungreased. Do not grease the sides of the pan.
2. Sift the flour, cocoa, baking soda, baking powder, and salt into a large bowl. Add the sugar, cinnamon, and cayenne, and whisk to combine.

3. In another large bowl, whisk the eggs, milk, oil, and vanilla until combined. Gradually add the wet ingredients to the dry ingredients and whisk until there are no lumps and the batter is smooth. Ask an adult to help carefully pour in the boiling water and stir until combined.

4. Pour the batter into the prepared pan. Bake in the center of the oven until a wooden skewer inserted in the center comes out clean and the cake bounces back when lightly pressed, about 25 to 30 minutes.

5. Meanwhile, make the tres leches: In a large bowl, combine the evaporated milk, condensed milk (setting 3 tablespoons aside for the whipped cream), heavy cream, and vanilla extract and whisk to combine. Cover with plastic wrap and refrigerate if not using immediately.

6. Ask an adult to help remove the cake from the oven with oven mitts, and let it stand for 10 minutes. Run a butter knife between the cake and the inside edges of the pan to separate. Cool completely.

7. Once cool, while the cake is still in the pan, use a skewer or a fork to poke small holes through the

cake to the bottom, about an inch apart. Slowly spoon some of the tres leches over the top of the cake, giving it time to soak in. Once the liquid is absorbed, repeat until all the tres leches is used. (Toward the end, the tres leches will pool at the edges, but don't worry; it will be absorbed while in the fridge.) Cover the cake with plastic wrap and refrigerate for at least 5 or 6 hours, preferably overnight.

8. When ready to serve, make the whipped cream: Add the reserved condensed milk along with the cream, vanilla, and cinnamon to the bowl of an electric mixer. Beat on medium high until the cream has doubled in volume, forms soft peaks, and is light and fluffy. Spread the cream onto the cake, then decorate the top with the strawberries and sprinkle with cinnamon. Serve from the pan.